S0-CFI-398

Calvin Williams

To my husband John and daughter Jenna. And to all my nieces and nephews, big and small, who fill my life with love. Also, a huge thank you to my dear friend Liz whose talent made this all possible.

www.mascotbooks.com

The Adventures of Leighton: It's Potty Time

©2019 Celeste Williams. All Rights Reserved. No part of this publication may be reproduced, stored in a retrieval system or transmitted in any form by any means electronic, mechanical, or photocopying, recording or otherwise without the permission of the author.

For more information, please contact:
Mascot Books
620 Herndon Parkway, Suite 320
Herndon, VA 20170
info@mascotbooks.com

Library of Congress Control Number: 2018913355

CPSIA Code: PRT0118A
ISBN-13: 978-1-64307-345-3

Printed in the United States

The Adventures of Leighton
It's Potty Time

By Celeste Williams

Illustrated by Liz Macchio

"I want to be a big kid! I want to go on the school bus," says Leighton.

"Soon, honey. First you need to go on the potty like a big girl," says Daddy. "That means no more diapers."

Leighton notices she's the only
one who wears diapers.

Raja doesn't wear diapers.

Mommy and Daddy don't wear diapers.

When she goes to Daddy's work no one wears diapers.

No one wears diapers at Mommy's work either.

The next morning Mommy and Daddy have a surprise for Leighton. "Close your eyes," they say as they walk her to the bathroom. "Now open them."

"It's my very own potty!" shouts Leighton.

Leighton is so excited she jumps right on it. "First you need to take off your diaper," chuckles Mommy.

"Oops!" laughs Leighton.

Leighton jumps up and runs to play. "Wait!" says Daddy. "First you need to wash your hands after you use the potty."

"Good work," says Daddy.
"Now run off and play!"

"It's been a while, Leighton. Let's try the potty again," says Mommy. "Raja will watch your toys till we get back."

Leighton runs to the
bathroom but by the
time she gets there,
uh-oh!

"That's okay,
accidents happen."

"Mommy has to go to work," says Mommy. "Let's try the potty again before we get in the car."

"Yay for Leighton!" cheers Mommy. "Time to flush and wash our hands."

Leighton gets a special sticker and a cup of her favorite berries for the car ride.

"Let's call Daddy when we get to Mémère's and tell him what a big girl you are for going on the potty," says Mommy.

"Yay!" cheers Leighton.

When Daddy picks Leighton up after work, he is so proud of his little girl. He gives her a big hug and another sticker. "Let's call Gramma E and tell her the news!"

Leighton loves having her own potty.
Sometimes she sits on it and reads and
reads while she waits to go.

Sometimes when Leighton goes on the potty, everyone celebrates together.

Leighton is a big girl now. She even wears big girl pants.

"When I'm old enough to go to school, I'll be ready because I'm a big girl now!"

The End

Hurray for

_____ !

No more diapers for me!
I'm a big girl now!

About the Author

Celeste Williams is a first time author who lives on Long Island, New York, with her husband John and daughter Jenna. Her great-niece Leighton inspired her to put pen to paper to chronicle this big milestone in her little life, with many more to come!